CW00847493

This book belongs to....

.....Seth...!.....................

MERRY CHRISTMAS 2018
love Autie Zona x.

For Alba & Nico

Published in association with Bear With Us Productions
for Amazon KDP Publishing.

NOAH'S SHARK

Written By

CLARE THOMPSON

Illustrated By

RICHIE T. EVANS

The children had a 'Show and Tell'
In Noah's class at school.
And Noah was excited,
He'd brought something really cool!

So when it got to Noah's turn,
He said, "I'll show you Mark."
And all the other children screamed...

As Noah had a **shark!**

"You cannot bring a shark to school,"
Said teacher, Mrs Rome.
"Okay," said Noah looking sad,
"I'd better take him home."

Noah picked Mark up and then
They travelled on the bus.
It took them ages to get home,
They caused a lot of fuss.

Sharks should be in water,
He was getting rather hot.
So Noah put him in the pond,
And Mark liked that a lot.

But Noah's Daddy shouted "Oi!"
As Mark's tail gave a swish,
"Please get that shark out of my pond,
He's eating all my fish!"

So Mark and Noah took a stroll,
Down to the local park,
But they caused chaos there as well,
As dogs began to bark.

Then Noah had a great idea,
He had been such a fool!
Mark would love a little dip,
Down at the swimming pool.

As soon as Mark got in the pool,
Everyone got out.
They stood there, silent, dripping wet,
And too afraid to shout.

Then one old lady got in and
Began to swim along.
Everyone watched silently,
She knew something was wrong.

She then said to the lifeguard,
"I think you should be told.
I did not enjoy my swim today,
The water's far too cold."

She hadn't even seen the shark,
Which made the lifeguard laugh.
But it was time for Noah to,
Go home and run a bath.

Once Mark was tucked up in the tub,
And it was after dark,
Noah sat down with his Dad,
To talk about the shark!

"I'm afraid that Mark can't live here.
He is too big for the house,
And every time he comes downstairs,
Your Mum shrieks like a mouse."

The next day Noah and his Mum,
Took Mark down to the zoo.
There he had the space to swim,
As he sure loved to do.

"Now Noah," said the zoo keeper,
"As you brought Mark to me,
Anytime you want to see him,
You can come for free."

Noah went home happy,
As he knew that Mark was well.
But now he had nothing to take,
To his next 'Show and Tell.'

So as he went to bed that night,
He made a secret wish.
And by his bed when he woke up...

There was a new **goldfish**!

Printed in Great Britain
by Amazon